Provincetown

Truro

Wellfleet

the
HILL

Alex's
Home

Cape Cod
National
Seashore

PETERS POND

Eastham

Brewster

Orleans

Dennis

Nickerson
State Forest

Barnstable

C·A·P·E   C·O·D

Chatham

Hyannis

S Yarmouth

www.mascotbooks.com

The Tales of ALEX the Cape Cod Ant: The Vacation

© 2016 W. M. Burnett
Illustrations © 2016 Terry Kole

Contact ALEX at:
thetalesofalexthecapecodant@yahoo.com
or visit his website:
www.thetalesofalexthecapecodant.com

For more information, please contact:
Mascot Books
560 Herndon Parkway #120
Herndon, VA 20170
info@mascotbooks.com

Library of Congress Control Number:
2016913848

CPSIA Code: PRT1016A
ISBN: 978-1-63177-550-5

Printed in the United States

First Edition 2016

TO: Liam & Lucas

Love, Auntie Bubba

W.M. Burnell 12/2020

The Tales of
ALEX
the Cape Cod Ant

We were having so much fun,
and then Alex wanted....

the
Vacation

Written by W.M. Burnett

Illustrated by Terry Kole

To my long, lost son Joshua,
who is now in my life again.
~ Bill Burnett

To my grandson, Parker.
Every day that I painted this book I was awaiting your arrival.
I can't wait to hold you and read it to you!
~ Terry Kole

One morning,
as Alex was laying on the beach,
an idea came into his head.

Wouldn't it be nice to go on a vacation?

Alex had never been on a vacation before.

He didn't even know where he would like
to go or even **how** to go on vacation!

Then Alex thought maybe his friend would
know about vacations.

So he went to see his best friend,
Lotta the Lady Bug.

"Hi Lotta, I was wondering if
you could help me plan a vacation?"

But Lotta had never been
on a vacation either,
so she couldn't offer much help!

She did remember that Casey the Cricket
had gone on a vacation last year
with his family to a wonderful place
called "The Hill."

She said that The Hill was about the cleanest, warmest part of Peters Pond there ever was.

Alex and Lotta walked over to
Casey's house and knocked on the door.

They had to knock and knock
again and again!

After a while, Casey answered and said,
"Come back later! I'm sleeping!"

But Alex and Lotta said,
"Please come out,
this is very important!"

Finally, Casey the Cricket opened the door.

His eyes were half shut.

"I need my sleep, you know!

What is so important?" he asked.

Lotta said, "You have to help us!

Alex wants to go on a vacation and

I want to go with him!"

Casey perked right up!
His eyes were now wide open as he said,
"VACATION!
I LOVE VACATIONS!
I want to come, too!
Where are we going to go?"

Alex spoke up and said,
"The Hill, of course!"

Casey said excitedly,
"I was there last year.
It was wonderful!"

The three of them sat down and started to plan out their vacation.

First they had to find a way there,
but no one had any idea which direction to walk!

Alex asked Casey if he could lead the way,
but Casey couldn't remember
how to get there either.

Then, Casey remembered that his friend,
Molly the Moth, had also been to The Hill before.
"She'll remember!" shouted Casey.
"She doesn't forget anything!"

Alex, Lotta, and Casey decided to
walk over to Molly's house.
Molly lived just down the path,
not very far from Casey's house.

So the three friends started on their way.

All of a sudden Alex said, "I'm hungry!"
and asked if they could eat
before they got to Molly's.
Lotta and Casey thought that
was a good idea
because they were hungry, too!

The three friends walked over
to an old oak tree
where each of them found
tasty pieces of fungus and leaves.

After they filled their stomachs,
they started toward
Molly's house again.

When they arrived, Casey knocked on the door,
but there was not a sound.
"I guess no one's home," Alex said.

Lotta spoke up and said, "Try knocking again."

So Casey knocked again but still no sound came
from the home.
Casey couldn't believe Molly wasn't there
and said, "I'll look out back."

Casey walked out back and found her working
in the garden, then went to get Alex and Lotta.
All three walked up to Molly.
She was so busy working in her garden and humming,
she didn't even notice them.
After a few seconds, Alex said, "Hi!"
Well, she jumped a foot in the air!

"Oh, my, we're sorry for scaring you,"
said Lotta.

Molly landed on her six little feet and said, "Oh, it's you, Casey! You gave me quite a scare sneaking up on me like that!"

"Oh, I'm sorry.
I came over with my two friends, Lotta and Alex.
We want to know how to get to The Hill.
Could you tell us?"

Molly said, "The Hill! I love that place!
Do you think I could go, too?"

All three said at once,
"YES!
That would be great!"

So the four of them started walking
toward The Hill.
After a while Alex said,
"I'm hungry again!"
Not only was he hungry, but he was tired too.
By the time he and his friends had finally
started on their way, it was late and getting dark.
Alex noticed the sun was setting.
He didn't like to be out at night
and was getting nervous.

Alex asked the others if they
wanted to turn around
and Molly said, "Why?"

Alex said,
"It's late, and we're not at The Hill,
and I'm scared!"

Molly said, "Alex, look up!
The Hill is right in front of you!"
Alex looked up, but it was so dark now
that he couldn't see a thing.
Then, all of a sudden, a small light came on.
It was the light for a sign that read
"The Hill."

They had finally made it!
It was late,
so they found twigs and pieces of leaves
and made their beds
and went to sleep.

In the morning,
Alex went swimming with Lotta.
Alex said, "Casey and Molly were right!
The water is so clean and warm!"
The two friends swam and were having fun,
but something was wrong...

Alex was homesick.
He asked Lotta if they could
head back home soon.

As they were coming out of the water,
they noticed Casey the Cricket running
in and out of the water and splashing Molly.
Molly moved away from Casey and said to Alex,
"I'm homesick, too!"

The four friends decided to head home,
but not before Alex said once again,
"I'm hungry!"

The four friends had a nice picnic
on The Hill and
then went home together.

ALEX is the nicest young ant you will ever meet!
He lives in Vacationland on Cape Cod. Visitors come from
all over the world just to enjoy a week or two in ALEX's
neighborhood.

But ALEX and his friends want to go on a vacation, too.
The question is WHERE?

In this adventure ALEX's group of friends keeps
growing...and everyone wants to go on vacation with
ALEX!

W.M. Burnett (Bill, as his friends call him) continues
his enchanting series with his second book, *The Vacation*.
In this adventure, you'll find ALEX doing what Bill has done
for the past fifteen years: vacationing on Peters Pond.

Bill is giving ALEX another address on Main Street in
Plymouth, Massachusetts at the new **Windemere
Gift & Book Shoppe.**
Come in and say hi and get your books signed!

Terry Kole is ALEX's favorite artist.
He asked her to illustrate this second story in his series
of adventures. He thinks she makes him look good!
Terry visits ALEX at Peters Pond to look at things from
his point of view.

Every day she clears off the breakfast table and turns it
into a magical world where her imagination goes free
and her paints go flying!

CAPE COD BAY

Cirde all the towns and beaches you have visited on or near Cape Cod!

Plymouth

Myles Standish
State Forest

MASSACHUSETTS

Sandwich

JOINT
BASE
CAPE
COD

Mashpee

Osterville

Falmouth